02 12

Detail from *Birthday (L'anniversaire)*, 1915

Self-Portrait with Seven Fingers: The Life of Marc Chagall in Verse

J. Patrick Lewis & Jane Yolen

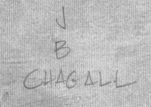

Text copyright © 2011 J. Patrick Lewis and Jane Yolen   Artwork permissions: © Artists Rights Society (ARS), New York/ADAGP, Paris / Collection Stedelijk Museum, Amsterdam / Solomon R. Guggenheim Founding Collection, by Gift (37.438)   Photographs by Getty Images (Henry Barreuther/Hulton Archive, Pierre Boulat/Time & Life Pictures, Hulton Archive), Heritage-Images (Russian Look), Magnum Photos (Philippe Halsman)   Published in 2011 by Creative Editions   P.O. Box 227, Mankato, MN 56002 USA   Creative Editions is an imprint of The Creative Company   Designed by Rita Marshall   All rights reserved   No part of the contents of this book may be reproduced by any means without the written permission of the publisher   Printed in Italy

Library of Congress Cataloging-in-Publication Data   Lewis, J. Patrick. Self-portrait with seven fingers: the life of Marc Chagall in verse / by J. Patrick Lewis and Jane Yolen. Includes bibliographical references. ISBN 978-1-56846-211-0.   1. Chagall, Marc, 1887–1985—Juvenile poetry. 2. Artists—Russia (Federation)—Biography—Juvenile poetry. 3. Children's poetry, American/I. Yolen, Jane. II. Title. PS3562.E9465S45 2011   811'.54—dc22   2009034767

CPSIA: 120110 PO1409   First edition 9 8 7 6 5 4 3 2 1

Detail from *Over Vitebsk*, 1914

Marc Chagall as a young man, 1915

Table of Contents

Detail from *Double Portrait with a Glass of Wine*, 1917

Maternity

Jane Yolen

The soft summer night is rent
by a long, single wail.
Uncles, aunts, the new father cry
L'chaim, to life.
They lift glasses glowing with schnapps:
May he be a herring merchant like his father,
a fiddler like his grandfather and uncle.
May his name be a blessing.
His mother holds the newborn close.
"May he always be happy in his work."
Still blind with birth, the infant
smells the colors around him:
the cobalt of his mother's eyes,
the pink of her neck,
the pitchblende of her hair,
the white of her milk.

Marc Chagall was born Moishe Shagal (with *shagal* meaning "to stride ahead, make progress" in Russian) on July 7, 1887, in Vitebsk, a Russian city whose population was half Jewish. Marc's childhood was happy yet humble. The eldest of nine children, he would not follow the trade of his father, a laborer in a herring factory. His love for his parents was never in doubt, though his father's working class life was a bit of an embarrassment. Marc was, as he would later admit, his mother's son. He learned the violin, painted, and wrote poetry. But his parents never wanted him to become an artist—a profession, they believed, that would not afford him a decent living.

L'chaim: the most common Jewish toast, which means "To life!"

Detail from *Maternity*, 1912–13

Maternity, 1912–13. Oil on canvas, 193 x 116 cm. Stedelijk Museum, Amsterdam.

I and the Village, 1911. Oil on canvas, 192.1 x 151.4 cm. The Museum of Modern Art, New York.

I and the Village

J. Patrick Lewis

I hailed a milkmaid standing on her head

I saw a cow a-milking in a cow's head

I watched a peasant off to canvass tillage

I met the very universe in a village

I spied a blossom sprig, a tree of life

I loved Vitebsk in glory and in strife

I scanned a multitude of images, with mirror

I etched a dream and strove to make it clearer

I solved the riddle imagined by a child

I sketched a field, geometry gone wild

I knew myself, white lips, my face in green

I drew the cow's contentment in between

More than a thousand years old, the city of Vitebsk, now part of Belarus, lies near the Russian and Latvian borders. The town—barren, mud-splattered, and decaying—was magnificent in Chagall's eyes. Even the most nondescript peasants, animals, shops, and synagogues were recurring muses as the boy began to nurse his artistic tendencies, and he felt at one with the tiny universe of his hometown. "The soil that nourished the roots of my art was Vitebsk," he wrote.

Detail from *I and the Village*, 1911

Over Vitebsk

J. Patrick Lewis

When I was nine and ten,
I tried to catch the moon,
Not as a fiddler on the roof
Like my grandfather
Or Uncle Zoussy,
But as an artist in the sky.
My cloudy chariot was bound
To glimpse the grandeur,
Though I was nothing more
Than a tattered sack
Of brushes making short
Journeys into wonder.

If ever there was a dreamer, it was Chagall. He seemed to know from his youngest years that he wanted to be an artist. A grade-school friend introduced him to tracing pictures, and an astonished Chagall believed at first that such an activity might be unlawful! His earliest drawings made obvious to everyone that he possessed a prodigious gift. In his late teens, he briefly studied painting with a Vitebsk artist, Yehuda Pen. From Pen, Chagall received a respectable education in the traditions of classical art, and yet his heavily modernist work turned his teacher's world upside down in its abandonment of realistic figures and perspectives.

Over Vitebsk, 1914. Oil on canvas, 71 x 92.2 cm. Art Gallery of Ontario, Toronto.

The Violinist

Jane Yolen

Oh, Uncle, play me a communion,

on your *kishefdik* violin

as you dance in big boots on the rooftop.

Let me sway with you in shoes of fire

on the streets of Lyozno, Ekaterinoslav, Vitebsk,

and in all the little *shtetls* where men dance together

and women envy our excess.

There is something heroic about that dance,

every one of us making our way in song

up the long road to the throne of G-d.

The violinist depicted in this painting is Chagall's uncle, who was a Chasid, or member of a Jewish sect that communed with God through ecstatic music. As a boy, Chagall thought his uncle was *kishefdik*, for the violinist often sat cross-legged on the roof playing his strings. That fiddler on the roof image would later inspire the famed Broadway musical.

Going to St. Petersburg at age twenty to study painting, Chagall said, "Terror gripped me. How could I manage to feed myself, since I'm good for nothing but perhaps to draw?" He wrote of his days there, "My means did not allow me to rent a room; I had to be content with corners of rooms. I did not even have a bed to myself." He found inspiration in the city, which was blooming with symbolism and poets, and yet Chagall painted what he'd loved longest and knew best—the little Jewish village where he'd grown up.

kishefdik: Yiddish for "magical" or "charmed by a magic spell"
shtetls: Jewish villages, often those just outside of big towns
G-d: the way some observant Jews spell the Lord's name

The Violinist, 1909. Oil on canvas, 188 x 158 cm. Stedelijk Museum, Amsterdam.

My Fiancée in Black Gloves

Jane Yolen

"I was surprised at his eyes,
they were so blue as the sky,
and oblong, like almonds,"
Bella writes, and having written,
falls in love, she so young and rich,
and he but a poor apprentice,
working for a Russian painter
he will one day eclipse,
a sun over Bakst's pale moon.
Did she know how he would rise

like an angel into the sky
on that first day they met,
having tea at Teja's house,
or the next time on the bridge
when he and Teja walked the dog,
and Marc's curly hair spilling
out from under his hat.
Or did she just fall in love
with the surprise of his blue eyes?

Chagall met Bella Rosenfeld, the daughter of a wealthy jeweler, in 1909 at her friend Teja's home. At the time, Chagall was a poor apprentice to painter and scene designer Leon Bakst. Shortly after Chagall and Bella met, they became engaged, and he painted *My Fiancée in Black Gloves*. In 1910, at the age of twenty-three, Chagall left Vitebsk for Paris, thanks to an academic grant. There he made many friends, including writer Blaise Cendrars. Despite his immediate and abiding affection for the City of Lights, Chagall could scarcely endure the distance that separated him from Bella for nearly four years. He returned to Vitebsk in 1914, and within a year, he and Bella were married. In his autobiography, *My Life*, he wrote, "Dressed all in white or black, she seemed to float over my canvases, for a long time guiding my art. I never finish a picture or an engraving without asking for her 'yes' or 'no.'"

My Fiancée in Black Gloves, 1909. Oil on canvas, 88 x 65.1 cm.
Kunstmuseum Basel, Basel, Switzerland.

In his autobiography, *My Life*, Chagall wrote, "Dressed all in white or black, she seemed to float over my canvases, for a long time guiding my art. I never finish a picture or an engraving without asking for her 'yes' or 'no.'"

Detail from *My Fiancée in Black Gloves*, 1909

Birthday

Jane Yolen

Which is better, a birthday kiss
from my almost bride,
a bouquet of summer flowers,
or to float joyously with her
over the bright red floor
and out the open window,
called by blue sky, white clouds,
meadows dotted with colors
as bright and various as G-d's eyes?

The years 1914 and 1915 were important
ones for Chagall. He had his first one-man
show in Berlin in 1914, and in 1915, he was
married. On his birthday, just days before
their wedding, Bella gave him a bouquet.
Later, she wrote: "[W]e lifted ourselves easily
together ... and floated ... [from] the window ... over meadows filled with flowers...."
But World War I was raging, and Chagall, un-
able to escape military service to his homeland, began a clerical job in the War Economy
Office in St. Petersburg. Although he hated
the job, it enabled him to meet many influen-
tial poets and writers, including Vladimir
Mayakovsky.

Birthday (*L'anniversaire*), 1915. Oil on cardboard, 81 x 100 cm.
The Museum of Modern Art, New York.

Double Portrait with a Glass of Wine

Jane Yolen

Bella carries me on her hands,
as Papa used to say of Mama,
so devoted to our small family
she could tote us like an old rag peddler
bent double with his heavy sacks of *shmatas*
through the rough streets of the city,
never feeling the weight.
All I have to give in return
are these scribbles full of color and love,
which are not heavy at all,
but Bella thinks they are enough.

Bella was the great love of Chagall's life. He painted her and their daughter Ida (born in 1916) over and over, as in *Double Portrait with a Glass of Wine*. Here his wife holds the artist aloft, while his angel Ida hovers over his head. This work shows the family living in Vitebsk, where the River Dvina—pictured below the figures—flowed.

In early 1920, just over a year after World War I's end, the Chagalls left for Moscow, where Marc had been commissioned to paint murals for the State Jewish Theater. Although he'd been named a commissar for art in Vitebsk, his connection with the new Soviet Union was doomed from the outset. His work did not celebrate the recent "glorious Russian Revolution," and so the government considered him a "non-person." The Chagalls longed to leave the Soviet Union and go to western Europe, where Marc would not have to promote a national agenda and where a Jewish painter could be celebrated. But it would be two more years before the family received permits to go.

shmatas: Yiddish for "rags" or "ill-treated clothing"

Double Portrait with a Glass of Wine, 1917. Oil on canvas, 233 x 136 cm.
Musée National d'Art Moderne, Paris.

Paris Through the Window, 1913. Oil on canvas, 135.8 x 141.4 cm.
Solomon R. Guggenheim Museum, New York.

Paris Through the Window

J. Patrick Lewis

My window opens to you, Paris!
Inhabit my brushes, dine on my canvas.
I throw back the curtains on your *boulangerie's*
aroma of fresh baguettes enticing the sky,
your left bank bistros, your Champs-Élysées,
that double-headed man looking both ways,
his heart in his hands, your man-faced cat
observing the scattered mice of lights,
your parachutist flying in his triangle hat,
your upside-down-bound-for-nowhere train,
the bowl of you, hollowed out by the Seine,
your eyeful tower, the couples thrilling
to every second of a horizontal life.

I paint you with blood and fire,
with eyelids closed, only my soul to see.
Come, mesmerize my heart across exotic
islands of the never-to-be-forgotten.

The Chagalls were finally allowed to leave their homeland in 1922. They journeyed first to Germany and then to Paris, which Chagall called his "second Vitebsk." He wrote, "My art needs Paris just as a tree needs water." During his earlier stay in Paris, he had created a body of work both wondrous and visionary. Images like those of the double-headed man in *Paris Through the Window* predated surrealism by nearly a decade and made Chagall one of the movement's pioneers. Surrealistic art exploded in 1920s Paris and consisted of work that was magical, surprising, and full of strange elements.

boulangerie: a French bakery specializing in breads
Champs-Élysées: perhaps the most well-known avenue in Paris

Detail from *Paris Through the Window*, 1913

Self-Portrait with Seven Fingers

J. Patrick Lewis

Today I make a work of art,
A red-and-orange wonderland,
By seven-fingered sleight of hand—
Let ambiguity play a part.

I stand the Eiffel Tower there,
Beyond the window of my room,
To let that monumental bloom
Create the necessary air

Of majesty, which represents
Oddly its counterpoint: lush dreams
Of home. I take these two extremes,
The margins of experience,

Allowing them to guide my hand—
This weird, improbable device
For resurrecting paradise—
So everyone might understand.

Self-Portrait with Seven Fingers is one of a series of large figure paintings that show Chagall wrestling with the possibilities of cubism—an art movement that became fashionable in the early 1900s—his life in Paris, and his longing for home in Russia. This piece, along with *The Violinist* and *Pregnant Women* (both produced in 1913), were purchased in 1914 by a collector for 900 francs (equal to approximately $3,930 in modern currency). That year, the showing of almost all of Chagall's Paris works at Der Sturm Gallery in Berlin marked the genesis of his worldwide fame. For the next 20 years, the avid interest of German collectors provided him with a lucrative source of income.

To do something "with seven fingers" is a Yiddish expression meaning to do it well or adroitly. In this piece, Chagall is shown painting one of his own works, *To Russia, Asses and Others*. Across the top, he has written in Yiddish the words "Paris" and "Russia."

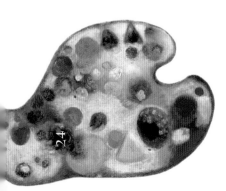

Detail from *Self-Portrait with Seven Fingers*, 1913–14

Self-Portrait with Seven Fingers, 1913–14. Oil on canvas, 128 x 107 cm.
Stedelijk Museum, Amsterdam.

The Promenade

J. Patrick Lewis

Vitebsk, my beloved village of goats and herring,
of small wooden houses and men with violins, is
mud-made of muted browns and greens.

Saint Petersburg, city of pickled cabbage, stagnant water,
and stifling granite, lays claim to Catherine the Great on
a palace palette embarrassingly blue.

Paris, City of Lights and scarlet nights, imagines
itself the patron of color to those it shelters,
people who believe that color is their reward
for not being born elsewhere.

New York, kaleidoscope of the world, red and
amber carnival of the senses, dares anyone to find
the gritty soul beneath her glitter petticoats.

In desperation we are all drawn to the light.
But why isn't everyone painting in purple?

"There's never been anybody since [Pierre-Auguste] Renoir who has the feeling for light that Chagall has," Pablo Picasso once said. "[W]hen [Henri] Matisse dies, Chagall will be the only painter left who understands what color really is." Chagall himself wrote that "there is a single color … which provides the meaning of life and art. It is the color of love." Given Chagall's extensive use of purple, that might well have been his "color of love."

In *The Promenade*, Chagall swings Bella like a flag across Vitebsk. In his other hand, according to biographer Jackie Wullschlager, he "holds a small bird, a reference to the allegorical fantasy *The Blue Bird* by Maurice Maeterlinck (one of Bella's favorite writers), where the hero and heroine do not find true love until they return from their travels to their simple home."

The Promenade, 1917–18. Oil on canvas, 170 x 163.5 cm.
State Russian Museum, St. Petersburg, Russia.

Marc Chagall with Bella, early 1920s

The Nazis had even taken over Paris, home to the Chagalls for eighteen years. The family was desperate to escape when Marc was arrested in Paris. After he was released, thanks to measures taken by the United States Emergency Rescue Committee, the Chagalls crossed over the Pyrenees mountains on foot into Spain, then sailed to America. Settling in New York, Chagall made a living by painting scenery and designing costumes for ballets.

The Flying Horse

Jane Yolen

There is no arguing with soldiers,
no pleading while wearing the yellow star.
There is only escape: on the rails, in the air,
on foot across mountains, one by one by one,
leaving behind the camps where men in stripes
and women with shaved heads,
and the children—never forget the children—
rock to and fro with G-d's name on their lips.
So you leave behind the bistros of Paris,
soldiers lurking in every corner of the city;
leave behind a lifetime of work,
paintings of Vitebsk on every wall.
But Death, that old leveler,
can find you wherever you go,
even on a sledge pulled by a rooster,
even as you rise into the darkling skies.

By 1941, Europe was under the heel of Adolf Hitler's Nazi Germany. Identified by yellow stars, Jews were herded into ghettos and concentration camps. The Nazis had even taken over Paris, home to the Chagalls for eighteen years. The family was desperate to escape when Marc was arrested in Paris. After he was released, thanks to measures taken by the United States Emergency Rescue Committee, the Chagalls crossed over the Pyrenees mountains on foot into Spain, then sailed to America. Settling in New York, Chagall made a living by painting scenery and designing costumes for ballets. While he was living in America, two devastating events happened. In 1941, the Nazis destroyed Vitebsk, the town of which Chagall had written, "Only that land is mine, that lies in my soul." Then, in 1944, Bella died.

The Flying Horse, 1945. Oil on canvas, 50 x 70 cm.
Collection of Mr. and Mrs. Harry Abrams, New York.

While he was living in America, two devastating
events happened. In 1941, the Nazis destroyed
Vitebsk, the town of which Chagall had written,
"Only that land is mine, that lies in my soul."
Then, in 1944, Bella died.

Detail from *The Flying Horse*, 1945

Autoportrait

Jane Yolen

I take off my hat to you, Vava,

and my heart,

that had stopped beating after Bella's death.

Only promise not to straighten my studio

where clutter feeds the artist's life

better even than bread or herring or wine

Here—surrounded by canvas, books,

globules of dried paint like little jewels,

the ever-boiling samovar,

and sketches tacked to the wall

that flutter each time

you open the door, my heart—

here is the workshop of my soul.

Touch the clutter, and I will divorce you,

I will divorce you,

I will divorce you

who has brought me back to this life,

I swear.

After Bella's death from a viral infection, Chagall was overwhelmed with loss and for a year could not paint at all. In 1945, a young Englishwoman named Virginia Haggard took a position as his housekeeper and almost immediately became his lover. Five years later, Virginia left him, taking their son David with her.

Very soon after, Chagall met and married Valentina "Vava" Brodsky, a Ukrainian-born hat maker who worked in London. According to a 1965 *Time Magazine* article, she "brought order to his life," though he often threatened to divorce her if she tried to bring order to his *studio*. As Vava explained, "He divorces me many times a day." They would remain together until his death some thirty years later. In 1965, Chagall made a famous lithographic portrait of himself with Vava standing in the doorway, perhaps wanting to tidy things up.

Autoportrait, 1965. Lithograph, 70 x 50 cm.

The Tribe of Levi, 1960–62. Stained-glass window, 338 x 251 cm.
Synagogue of the Hadassah University Medical Center, Jerusalem, Israel.

The Tribe of Levi

J. Patrick Lewis

A man, at seventy,
awed by the subtlety of glass,
sees a luminous partition
revealing secrets of the sun,

And a child, tying her shoe
beside the pulpit, is stopped
by the plot of a picture-book
story written in air,

And a mother, taking stock
of her busy wisdom,
is immersed in the glow
of the Israelites on high,

And a widower, nodding
in the sleep of oceans,
awakens to the mystical world
of ancient ancestors beaming
down at him.

And the man, at seventy,
settles to the certainty
that his mind's eye has captured
the rapture of the world.

Stained-glass window art—which dates back to the eleventh century—requires not only a painter but an artisan to transmit the design to glass. In 1958, Chagall met Charles Marq, a master stained-glass craftsman. Marq would become the painter's closest friend and collaborator during the last half of Chagall's life. Perhaps their greatest achievements in the art form were the windows representing the twelve tribes of Israel—windows that *Time* hailed as "a revelation in glass." Chagall's stunning stained-glass art can be found the world over in churches and museums—but it is in only one Jewish synagogue, that of the Hadassah University Medical Center in Jerusalem, Israel. Such art bears out Chagall's belief that "[a]ll colors are the friends of their neighbors and the lovers of their opposites."

The Fall of Icarus

J. Patrick Lewis

There was a young man who believed he could fly
On a pair of wax wings to the sun in the sky—
An adventure confirming to all passersby
    The folly the lad was pursuing.

He flew to the clouds—here accounts disagree.
Some say his wings melted like butter as he
Descended headlong to an uncaring sea,
    As *Bruegel* imagined him doing.

But Chagall's Icarus is no seafaring lad.
He falls on the land of a rabble gone mad.
Some are happy he's failed, some unspeakably sad.
    Poor Icarus knows that he's dying.

A field separates them that's bitter blood-red:
Remorse stands to one side, but Evil has spread
Across the divide, now applauding the dead—
    The spectacle too mortifying.

Having left America for good in 1948, Chagall spent the last half of his life in various places in France. Some of his later paintings have been criticized for being too safe and predictable, too joyful or sentimental. Not so *The Fall of Icarus*, created when Chagall had reached the age of eighty-eight. Although he continued to make mosaics and stained-glass windows well into his nineties, the 1970s were a time of celebration for Chagall—from retrospective exhibitions of his work in major museums to honorary degrees from universities. A New York art dealer said, "He took so many commissions so that he will not have time to die." Yet in 1985, at his home in Saint-Paul-de-Vence, France, Chagall passed away at the age of ninety-seven.

Bruegel (Pieter the Elder): 16th century Flemish artist who painted *Landscape with the Fall of Icarus* in 1558

Detail from *The Fall of Icarus*, 1975

The Fall of Icarus, 1975. Oil on canvas, 213 x 198 cm. Musée National d'Art Moderne, Paris.

The authors benefited greatly from the following sources:

Alexander, Sidney. *Marc Chagall: A Biography*. New York: G. P. Putnam's Sons, 1978.

Baal-Teshuva, Jacob. *Marc Chagall 1887–1985*. Cologne: Taschen, 2008.

Bohm-Duchen, Monica. *Chagall*. London: Phaidon Press, 2001.

Chagall, Bella. *Burning Lights*. tr. by Norbert Guterman. New York: Biblio Press, 1996.

Chagall, Marc. *My Life*. tr. by Dorothy Williams. London: Peter Owen, 1965.

Crespelle, Jean-Paul. *The Love, the Dreams, the Life of Chagall*. tr. by Benita Eisler. New York: Coward-McCann, 1970.

Genauer, Emily. *Marc Chagall*. New York: Collins, 1957.

Harshav, Benjamin. *Marc Chagall and His Times: A Documentary Narrative*. Palo Alto, Calif.: Stanford University Press, 2004.

Kimmel, Eric A. *A Picture for Marc*. New York: Random House, 2007.

Wilson, Jonathan. *Marc Chagall*. New York: Schocken, 2007.

Wullschlager, Jackie. *Chagall: A Biography*. New York: Alfred A. Knopf, 2008.

Marc Chagall, 1960